THINGS YOU NEVER knew about DINOSAURS

Giles Paley-Phillips

illustrated by

Liz Pichon

Did you know that dinosaurs
Are still around today?
They didn't die off long ago,
They never went away.

On every street in every town
Perhaps next door to you,
Dinosaurs are doing things
You won't **believe** are true...

Dinosaurs play tennis.

They ride around on bikes.

They like to bounce on trampolines...

and go for hilltop hikes.

Dinosaurs love to play guitar,
To stomp their feet and sing.

They love to waltz and
cha cha cha
And do the Highland fling.

There are some things they **DON'T** like much,
The same as me and you:
Dinosaurs don't like doing sums...

or queuing for the loo.

You'll never see them brush their teeth
Or clean their dirty plates.
And when they should be fast asleep,
They're whizzing round on skates!

Some dinosaurs go up in space
To see the Moon and Mars.

Others go to Hollywood
And become big movie stars.

Dinosaurs sail the seven seas,

They trek from pole to pole...

And in the World Cup final
One scored the **winning goal.**

GO PTERODACTYL!

Yes, dinosaurs do amazing things,
It's all completely true.
But most of all,
their favourite thing...